MW00759858

A GOLDEN BOOK • NEW YORK

Special thanks to Sarah Buzby, Cindy Ledermann, Ann McNeill, Dana Koplik, Emily Kelly, Sharon Woloszyk, Tanya Mann, Julia Phelps, Rita Lichtwardt, Kathy Berry, Rob Hudnut, David Wiebe, Shelley Dvi-Vardhana, Michelle Cogan, Rainmaker Entertainment, and Walter P. Martishius

www.barbie.com
Published in the United States by Golden Books, an imprint of Random House Children's Books, a division of Random House, Inc., 1745 Broadway, New York, NY 10019, and in Canada by Random House of Canada Limited, Toronto.
randomhouse.com/kids
ISBN: 978-0-307-97676-5
Printed in the United States of America
10 9 8 7 6 5 4 3 2 1

Adapted by Kristen L. Depken

Based on the screenplay by
Steve Granat & Cydne Clark

Illustrated by Ulkutay Design Group

In the kingdom of Meribella, there lived a beautiful princess named Tori. She and her younger sisters, Meredith and Trevi, had many royal responsibilities. They had to attend balls and ceremonies, always poised and perfectly proper, and welcome royalty from other kingdoms. It was a lot of work.

Whenever they had a chance, the princesses would sneak off to play games and have fun.

Keira was a world-famous pop star who wrote songs, sang, and danced. She had millions of fans—including Princess Tori! Everyone loved Keira's exciting performances, which were filled with complex dance routines, laser lights, and even fireworks.

Keira loved being a pop star, but touring, greeting fans, and giving interviews didn't leave her much time for her true passion—writing songs.

Sometimes Princess Tori dreamed of being a famous pop star with a fun, music-filled schedule.

And Keira often dreamed of being a princess with a sweet, pampered life.

One day, Keira attended a royal reception at the palace. She had been invited to perform in a concert in honor of the kingdom's five hundredth anniversary. Princess Tori couldn't wait to meet her!

"I am absolutely your biggest fan ever!" exclaimed Tori as she shook Keira's hand.

Keira's bulldog puppy, Riff, wagged his tail excitedly at Tori's princess pup, Vanessa.

Keira was amazed by the regal surroundings. "Nice place you've got here," she said to Tori.

"Would you like a tour?" asked Tori. Before Keira could respond, the princess grabbed the pop star's hand and whisked her off.

The girls' first stop was Princess Tori's grand bedroom.

"When I was little, I always dreamed of being a princess," gushed Keira.

Tori offered her tiara to Keira to try on.

"I've got just the outfit to go with it!" said Keira. She pulled out a magical microphone and waved it around her head. A cloud of sparkles appeared—and Keira's outfit suddenly changed to match Tori's.

"Brilliant!" said Tori. "I have something like that, too." She took out a magical hairbrush and used it to change her hair to match Keira's. The girls then traded the microphone and the hairbrush and tried the magical powers on each other.

Moments later, the girls turned to look at each other. "You look just like me!" they said at the same time.

"Can you keep a secret?" asked Princess Tori. She led Keira down an ancient hallway and into a secret garden filled with bright, beautiful flowers and sparkling waterfalls. In the center grew a gardenia, its blossoms glittering with diamonds. Small garden fairies zipped back and forth, guarding and tending to the plant.

"Wow!" said Keira.

"This plant is the Diamond Gardenia," Tori explained. "The flower's roots spread all through the kingdom. Without it, Meribella would wither and die."

Using two tiny diamonds that had fallen from the sparkling flowers, the garden fairies made a star necklace for Keira and a heart necklace for Tori.

"These rock!" exclaimed Keira.

"We'll wear them as friendship necklaces," added Tori, "so we'll always remember today."

The girls didn't notice that Keira's greedy manager, Crider, was peering into the garden—and staring at the Diamond Gardenia. He planned to steal the plant during Keira's concert, when there would be no one around.

The next morning, Tori and Keira had a great idea—they decided to switch places for the day.

Keira taught Tori how to be a pop star and Tori taught Keira how to be a princess.

The girls switched pets too, so that Vanessa and Riff could help them in their new roles. They couldn't wait.

Princess Tori spent the morning practicing Keira's dance routine. She loved singing and dancing onstage. Tori knew the steps so well that none of the choreographers suspected she wasn't really Keira!

After breakfast, Keira, now in her princess best, took the royal carriage to a flower show. No one could tell she wasn't really Princess Tori!

Later that day, Tori and Keira talked about how much fun they'd had pretending to be each other.

"Too bad it's over," said Keira. "Unless . . . we want to keep it going one more day?"

"You're on!" replied Tori.

However, the next day didn't go as well as the first.

At the palace's dining table, Keira's manners were not very royal. Meredith and Trevi began to suspect that Keira wasn't really Princess Tori.

During rehearsal, Tori couldn't keep up with the new dance steps. She tripped and fell right in the middle of the stage.

Still disguised as Keira, Princess Tori took a walk through the kingdom. She found herself in a run-down area she had never visited before.

"Hey, you're Keira!" called a little girl. A group of children ran over to Tori, believing she was their favorite pop star.

"I really want to see your concert," said another girl. "But my dad says we can't afford it."

Tori's people needed her more than she had realized. It was her duty to help them.

Just then she had an idea—she would arrange for all the children of Meribella to see the concert for free!

At the palace, Keira played with Meredith and Trevi. They had a pillow fight and jumped on Tori's bed, bursting with giggles.

"Look how high we can fly!" cried a bouncing Trevi.

Keira had never felt so free. She was so happy that she was inspired to write a new song.

As Keira worked on her new song, the king walked into the room. He pulled her aside and told her that the Diamond Gardenia had been stolen!

"We'll find out who did this and get the plant back," said Keira. "I promise."

She tried calling the real Princess Tori—just as Tori was trying to call her!

The girls missed each other's calls.

Tori didn't know what to do. She was backstage preparing for the big concert that evening. If the real Keira didn't get there in time, Tori would have to perform in her place. She was terrified! But when Keira didn't arrive, Tori knew she had to go onstage. Keira's career depended on it.

Trembling with fear, Tori walked out in front of the cheering crowd, grabbed a guitar, and began to play and sing. Her voice was soft and shaky at first, but it grew stronger as she gained confidence. The audience loved her!

In the middle of the show, the lights of the kingdom began to flicker. Flowers wilted, and trees shed their leaves. Tori knew something was wrong.

"The Diamond Gardenia!" she cried and ran off the stage.

Tori headed to the palace. She ran straight into Keira. The girls switched places and then ran to find the Diamond Gardenia and save the kingdom.

A carriage rushed past the girls. Crider was inside—and he was holding the Diamond Gardenia!

"Excuse me, but I think that belongs to my kingdom!" cried Tori.

The girls took off after the passing carriage.

As the carriage sped away, Tori and Keira looked up at an overhead lantern cable. Realizing that Crider's carriage would be passing beneath it in just moments, the two friends grabbed hold of the cable.

"Three, two, one!" Tori counted. She and Keira slid down the cable like a zip line.

Tori landed right in front of the carriage, causing it to stop short.

"I'll take back that plant *and* the diamonds, Mr. Crider," she demanded.

Crider refused—until Keira dropped from the zip line into the carriage, knocking him to the ground.

"I've got it!" said Keira as she grabbed the Diamond Gardenia.

"Keep your crummy plant!" yelled Crider. "I've still got the diamonds!" Crider escaped but was soon caught by the palace guards.

Tori and Keira had no time to waste. They hurried back to the palace to replant the Diamond Gardenia, but it was no use.

"It's dead," Tori said sadly.

Suddenly, the girls remembered their diamond friendship necklaces.

"Seeds!" cried Keira.

Quickly, the friends planted the diamonds from their necklaces. The garden fairies flew over and watered them. The seeds immediately sprouted into two new glittering Diamond Gardenia plants!

Slowly, the kingdom came back to life.

Then the girls remembered where they were supposed to be.

"The concert!" they cried.

As they raced to the concert, Keira realized that although she'd had fun as a princess, she was happiest as a pop star, and she didn't want to disappoint her fans. And Princess Tori realized that she'd had fun as a pop star, but she was happiest as a princess. She had a kingdom to take care of.

The crowd went wild when both girls walked onstage.

"Please welcome my best friend, Her Royal Highness Princess Tori!" said Keira. The two best friends began to sing a beautiful song together.

The princess and the pop star put on an amazing show that no one would ever forget.